The ROLLER-COASTER RiDE

DAVID BROADBENT

Vincent and his grandma were zooming along
in a purple bus on their way to the beach.

"How about a ride on the roller coaster
when we arrive?" asked Grandma.

"That would be AMAZING!" said Vincent.

Vincent loved roller coasters.

They were so much fun!

"Don't get too excited!" warned Grandma.
"I haven't been there for ages.
It might not be there any more."

"I've heard some roller coasters go so fast your face goes all rubbery!"
laughed Vincent.

"Some roller coasters are so high they go up into space!" exclaimed Vincent.

"They can certainly be high," agreed Grandma. "But maybe not quite that high."

"Will the roller coaster go
upside down in a loop?"
asked Vincent.
"How come you don't fall out?
Do you hang upside down
like a bat?"

"No, they're perfectly safe," replied Grandma.
"You don't need to hang like a bat!"

"Will there be a carousel too?"
asked Vincent.

"Carousels spin
around ever so fast,"
explained Grandma.
"I don't want you
to get all dizzy!"

"What about bumper cars? They're really fun," suggested Vincent.

"We'll see. Let's just hope the roller coaster is still there," replied Grandma.

Vincent crossed his fingers.

"It will be AMAZING!" he announced.

He imagined flying around, up and down, super-fast on a thrilling ride.

The beach was busy when they arrived.
Some children were playing on the sand,
and the amusement park looked very exciting!

But there was a problem...

Funland was closed!

"Don't look so sad, Vincent,"
said Grandma.
"How about an ice cream instead?"

Vincent wasn't sure even an ice cream could make him happy again.

"What would you like?"
asked the ice-cream seller.

"I wanted a ride on the roller coaster," replied Vincent.
"But the amusement park is closed."

Vincent loved his ice cream – and the little park Grandma found!

There were so many rides
to choose from...

that he completely forgot
about the roller coaster.

And he found a really special ride back to the bus stop!

city

mountain bike trail

river

windmill

clock tower

cycle
track

lake

campsite

sports park

stone circle

wetlands